A MAGIC CIRC

IN THE ZOO

story by **JERRY LANE**
pictures by **BLAIR DRAWSON**

THEODORE CLYMER
SENIOR AUTHOR, READING 360

GINN AND COMPANY
A XEROX EDUCATION COMPANY

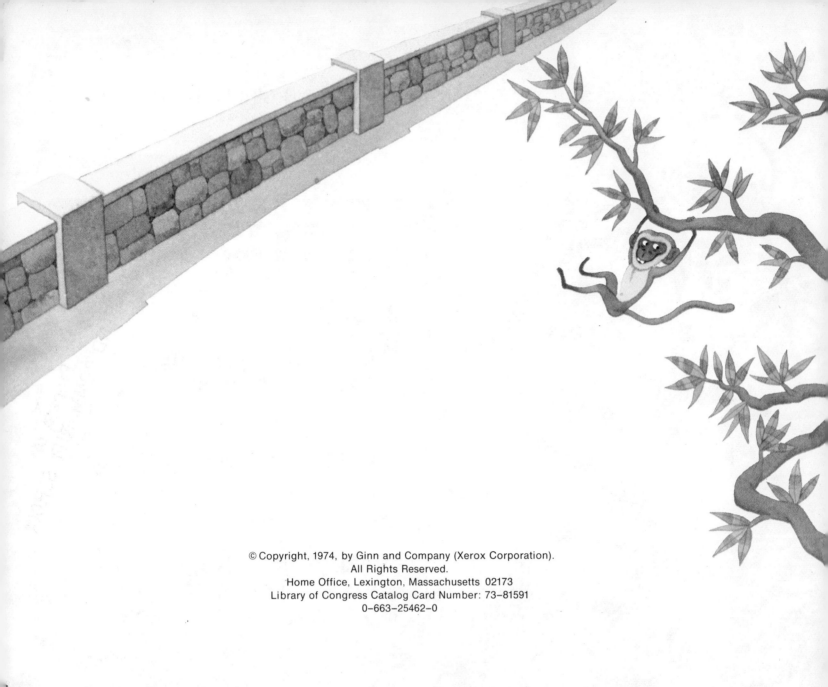

"Get up!" said the monkeys.

"Why?" said the lion.

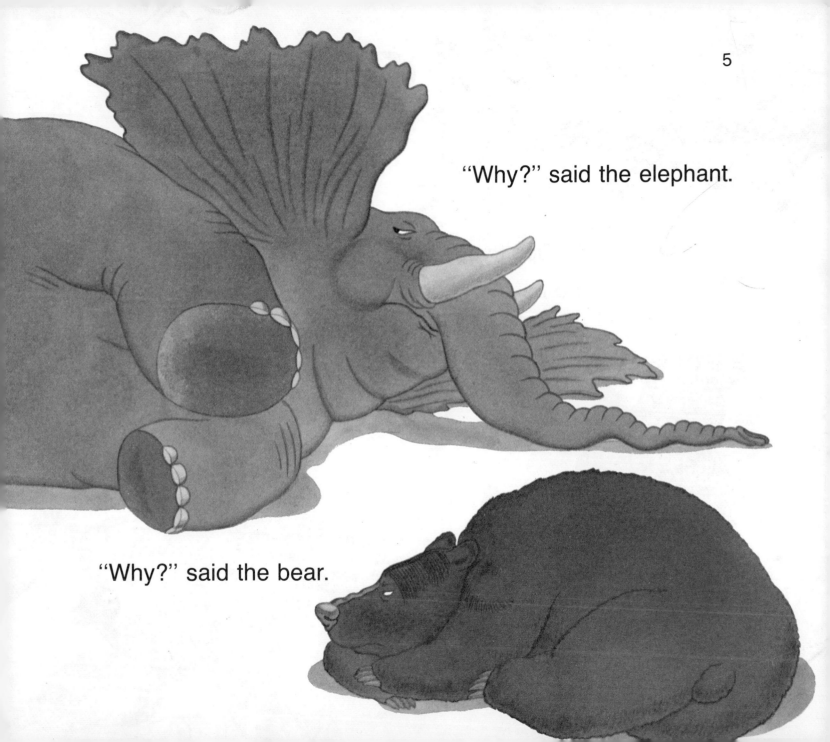

"Why?" said the elephant.

"Why?" said the bear.

"Don't you want to see
the boys and girls when they come
to the zoo?" said a big monkey.

"Yes-yes-yes," said the bear,
and the lion, and the elephant.

"Get up!" the bear said to the fox.

"Don't you want to see the boys
and girls when they come to the zoo?"

"I can't say that I do," the gruff old fox said.
"I don't like boys and girls."
And the fox did not get up.

"I like boys and girls.

They are funny," said the little monkey.

"And here they are."

The boys and girls and a man
walked into the zoo.

"Hello-hello-hello-hello-hello,"
said the monkeys.

"Hello," said the elephant.

"HelloooOOOOOOoooo," said the fox.

"Hello," said the bear.

"Hello," said the lion.

The boys and girls walked and walked.
They looked and looked at the animals.

And the animals looked
and looked at the boys and girls.

"Look!" the little monkey said.

The bear said, "This boy likes me."

"Look-look-look-look-look-look,"
said the monkeys.

Then the boys and girls
and the man walked out of the zoo.

"I like boys and girls,"
the little monkey said.
"I think boys and girls are funny."

"That's what I think," said the bear.

"That's what I think," said the elephant.

"That's what I think," said the lion.

But the gruff old fox
did not say a thing.

EFGHIJK 76
PRINTED IN THE UNITED STATES OF AMERICA